P9-CBR-666

The whisper of a fairy
The magic of its word
Will help those in the forest
Whenever it is heard

And when there is danger
Wherever there is need
A fairy's care and help
Will be there indeed

a min@dition book
published by Penguin Young Readers Group

Text copyright © 2008 by Simone Lindner
Illustrations copyright © 2008 by Christa Unzner
Original title: Luftelfe Tara
English text translation by Kathryn Bishop
Coproduction with Michael Neugebauer Publishing Ltd., Hong Kong.
Licensed by Margarete Steiff GmbH, Giengen, Germany
Rights arranged with "minedition" Rights and Licensing AG, Zurich, Switzerland.
All rights reserved.
This book, or parts thereof, may not be reproduced in any form without permission in writing
from the publisher, Penguin Young Readers Group, 345 Hudson Street, New York, NY 10014.
The scanning, uploading and distribution of this book via the Internet or via any other means without
the permission of the publisher is illegal and punishable by law. Please purchase only authorized
electronic editions, and do not participate in or encourage electronic piracy of copyrighted materials.
Your support of the author's rights is appreciated.
Published simultaneously in Canada.
Manufactured in Hong Kong by Wide World Ltd.
Typesetting in Frutiger, by Adrian Frutiger.
Color separation by Fotoriproduzione Grafiche, Verona, Italy.

Library of Congress Cataloging-in-Publication Data available upon request.

ISBN 978-0-698-40069-6

10 9 8 7 6 5 4 3 2 1
First Impression

For more information please visit our website: www.minedition.com

Also published in this series:

Aelin, the Water Fairy
Amar, the Earth Fairy
Runya, the Fire Fairy

Tara, the Air Fairy

by Simone Lindner
Illustrated by Christa Unzner
Translated by Kathryn Bishop

minedition

WITHDRAWN

ROCKFORD PUBLIC LIBRARY

"I don't want to get up," said Tara, the Air Fairy.
It was so cold that Tara's breath made frosty little clouds.
She pulled her dandelion-down blanket up over her ears.
But if she didn't get up, she'd miss so much!

She loved how the morning wind blew the night clouds away,
and the first sunbeams helped the little flower buds to open.

So Tara sprang lightly from her hammock.
It was icy cold under her feet.
She jumped into her clothes, moved her wings a bit, and then flew off, carried by the morning wind.

The meadow was still shiny from the morning dew, and in the shadow of a tree she saw two little flowers, still covered in frost, eagerly seeking the warm sunlight.
But the leaves covering them were just too heavy.
The little buds looked so weak and pale.
Tara tried with all her might to pull the heavy, frozen leaves away.
But there was no way. Her arms just weren't strong enough.
What could she do?

Tara held her arms wide and sang a fairy song.
Then like a spinning top she began dancing in
the wind.

She spun so quickly it warmed the air, and the
frost began to thaw.
Suddenly free, the two little flowers turned their
heads toward the warmth of the sun.
Tara landed next to them, a bit dizzy but smiling.
The air smelled of fresh grass, and she
could hear the bees buzzing, the tinkling
of tiny flower bells, and the rustling of
leaves.
She also heard a soft yet angry, "Oh, phooey!"
Tara got up but she didn't see anything.
The grumbling got louder.

Tara looked around and saw
something wiggling on the bark
of a tree above her.
She flew upward to the brown,
complaining whatever-it-was.
"Good morning," she said politely.
"Do you need help?"

"I don't know," said the brown thing. "The only thing
I know for sure is that I'm stuck here on a tree."
"However did you manage to get yourself stuck?" Tara asked.
"I have no idea," sniffed the little brown thing, wiggling about.

Tara made a swing on a branch of a tree so she could talk to
her new friend.

"Tell me everything," she said.

"I have such bad luck," said the brown thing.
"When I was born, I was little and fat, then I got big and fat.
  All I could do was crawl around, eat, and be afraid that
  something would eat me!"

"Oh, you poor thing," cried Tara. "Then what happened?"
"I can't really remember. I was so tired, and the birds kept
  chasing me. So I hid in this tree and fell asleep. I've been
  stuck here ever since."

Tara felt sorry for the whatever-it-was.
"My name's Tara, and you are…"
"Everyone just calls me Caterpillar,"
replied the thing.

Tara nodded, flew out of her swing, and began
pulling on the caterpillar. But it was really stuck!
She tried again, her little hands on the hard caterpillar shell.
"You are really stuck," she said.
The little caterpillar just looked at her with big sad eyes.
"Wait," she said. "Maybe I can try something else."
She flew back to her swing. Back and forth she rocked,
reciting magical words.

Ni nalla tulu !
I call for help !

Heart of a fairy, brave and true
Show me now what I must do
Give me an answer, help me see
How to set the caterpillar free.

"I've got it!" shouted Tara, laughing. "You were a caterpillar, but
you are about to become something quite different.

"You're just stuck in a cocoon. I can't pull it
from the tree, but together we can get you out,"
she said. "Relax and take slow, deep breaths."
Tara started to pull gently at the cocoon.
As the caterpillar finally began to come loose,
Tara asked, "Can you stamp your feet and flutter your
wings a little?"

"What feet? What wings?" asked the caterpillar.
Then, slowly, wings started to
emerge from the dark cocoon.
"Keep breathing deeply.
You need power in your
wings to fly."
"I don't understand,"
said the caterpillar, taking
deep breaths.
In a few minutes there
was a soft, crackling
sound, and two shimmering,
colorful wings unfolded.

"What a beautiful butterfly you are!" said Tara, clapping her hands. "A whole new life is about to begin for you. You're going to need a name. Hmmm, I have it! Edlothia! That means to blossom in my language."

"Now, follow me. I'll show you how to fly." Edlothia lifted off but tumbled in the wind behind Tara.
"This awful wind keeps pushing me around," she said. "How am I ever going to learn to fly?"
"The wind isn't awful," said Tara. "Don't forget we need the wind to breathe and smell… and to fly, of course. You'll learn. I'll show you a few tricks. You just need practice. You learn to fly by flying. Watch!"

Tara and Edlothia practiced and practiced. They flew high and low, fast and slow. They flew all around the meadow where the beautiful flowers had opened.

Edlothia was even able to land and drink sweet nectar
from the blossoms.

"Thank you, Tara," said Edlothia. "Flying is wonderful,
but it sure makes you tired." And she landed on a daisy
to rest.

Tara sat on another daisy and said, "Don't thank me.
You did very well. You'll be a great flyer with
a little patience and time.

But it's fun, isn't it!"

Suddenly a bright light filled the sky.
"That is exactly right, dear Tara," said a beautiful voice.
"You too have done your job well."

"*Bereth,* the Fairy Queen," whispered Tara as she made a
graceful curtsey.
The Queen glistened in her flowing white dress, sparkling with
the light of a thousand diamonds. Her long hair shone, and
her delicate wings shimmered with every color of the rainbow.

"Tara, you are a very special Air Fairy,"
said the Fairy Queen. "You have cared for
the plants and the animals for a long time.
I would now like to send you into the world of
human children. Are you ready to go?"

The little fairy was so surprised, she held her breath
for a moment.
Then her face lit up, and she nodded happily.
"Yes, I'm ready!" she exclaimed.
The Queen opened a shining white bud and
took out a mysterious gold ring.
"Tara, Air Fairy, I hereby present you with the magic
fairy ring, the ring of your element, air.

The ring will serve you
in the human world.
It will help you exchange
your secret messages, and it
will seal your friendships. When
it is placed on the ground, it will
create a large circle, and only those
who enter it will be able to see you,
to speak and dance with you.

"From now on you are to be a
friend and protector of a human child.
That child is reading this story and
is waiting for you."

Tara beamed and placed the ring
on her finger.

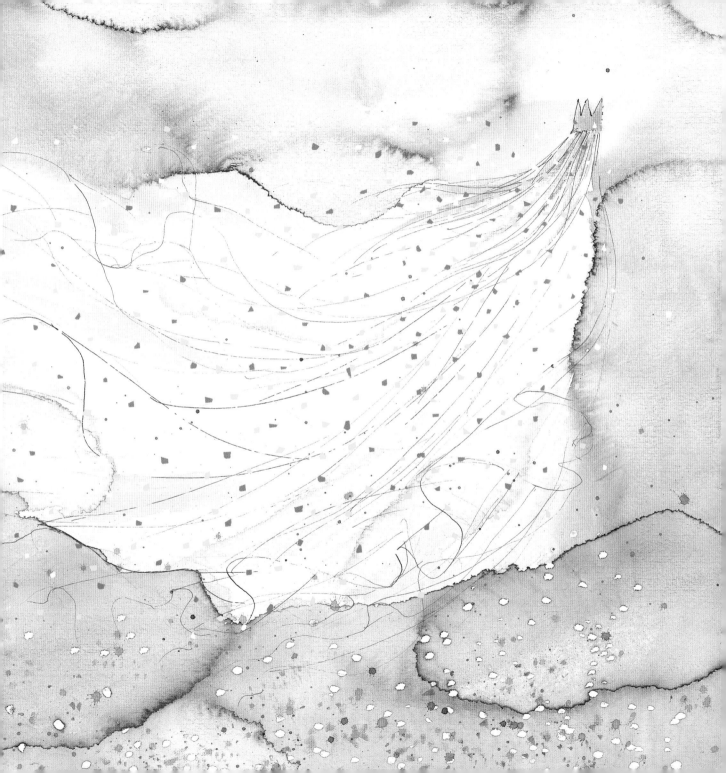

Then the shining light disappeared as suddenly as it had come. For Tara, the Air Fairy, a new adventure was about to begin…

Could her adventure be with *you?*

Which of the elements suits you best?

WATER and *Aelin* ⬦

1. imaginative
2. bubbly
3. creative
4. pure
5. lakes, rivers
6. sea, ocean
7. waves
8. waterfalls
9. raindrops, snowflakes
10. ice crystals
11. slide, float
12. swim

FIRE and *Runya* ⬦

1. fiery
2. warm-hearted
3. explosive
4. enthusiastic
5. full of energy
6. gives warmth
7. brings light in the darkness
8. sparkling
9. crackle
10. sun
11. fire light
12. firesides

EARTH and *Amar* ◯

1. rascal
2. steadfast
3. healing abilities
4. good-natured
5. rocks and stones
6. mountains and valley
7. forests and meadows
8. earth, trees, and roots
9. plants and flowers
10. digging
11. playing in the sand
12. all 4 seasons

Air and *Tara* ◇

1. happy
2. playful
3. quick-tempered
4. wind
5. storm
6. sky
7. clouds
8. flying with birds
9. soaring, floating
10. feeling free as a breeze
11. feeling light as a feather
12. pinwheels and kites

When you have finished the book and have discovered the wonders of the fairy, open this letter. It was written especially for you!